This book belongs to:

_____

For Brian Williams. J.W.

This paperback edition first published in 2016 by Andersen Press Ltd.
First published in Great Britain in 2014 by Andersen Press Ltd.,
20 Vauxhall Bridge Road, London SW1V 2SA.
Text copyright © Jeanne Willis, 2014. Illustrations copyright © Tony Ross, 2014.
The rights of Jeanne Willis and Tony Ross to be identified as the author
and illustrator of this work have been asserted by them in accordance with
the Copyright, Designs and Patents Act, 1988.
All rights reserved. Printed and bound in China.

1 3 5 7 9 10 8 6 4 2

British Library Cataloguing in Publication Data available.

ISBN 978 1 78344 156 3

Jeanne Willis

Tony Ross

BOA'S BAD BIRTHDAY

ANDERSEN PRESS

It was Boa's birthday.
It was going to be the best one ever.
Or so he hoped.

He invited his friends round.
They would all bring him wonderful presents.
Or would they?

Orang-utan's was enormous.
"Please don't let it be
what I think it is,"
thought Boa.
But it was...

...a piano!

Boa couldn't play it. He had no fingers.
"It's the thought that counts," said his mother.

Orang-utan clearly hadn't thought very hard,
but maybe Monkey had. He was clever.
Or was he?

His parcel looked **very** interesting...

"You'll love it!" said Monkey.

But Boa didn't.
It was a pair of...

...sunglasses!

"Everyone's wearing them," said Monkey.
But Boa wasn't. They kept slipping off.
He had no ears or nose.
"Thanks," said Boa. "They're lovely."

But, secretly, he was deeply disappointed.
"Third time lucky," said his mother.

Jaguar arrived with a neat package.
"I hope you like them!" he said.

Boa hoped so too.
He could hardly wait to unwrap it.

"I thought they'd be useful," said Jaguar.
But they weren't. They were...

...mittens!

"Do you like the colour?" asked Jaguar.
"It's my favourite," said Boa.

But what he really wanted to say was,
"Why buy me mittens? Are you mad?

I have no hands!"

But that would have been rude.
It was kind of his friends
to get him anything.
Perhaps Sloth's gift would
be more suitable.

But it wasn't. It was a...

...hairbrush!

"It's a very good one," insisted Sloth.

But it was no good for Boa.

He had no hair!

"Open my parcel," said Anteater.
"You'll have great fun with it!"

But Boa didn't.
It was a...

...football!

It was no fun at all!
Boa couldn't kick it.
He had no feet!

It was Boa's worst birthday ever.

All his gifts were rubbish.

And just when he thought things
couldn't get any worse...

"Dung Beetle's here!" said his mother.
"I bet her present is a pile of
You Know What," thought Boa.

And he was right!

But he was also wrong,
because in the dung ball, there was a seed.
And when it rained, it sprouted.

And it grew...

And it grew...

And it grew into...

...a beautiful tree!

It was the perfect present for a boa.
It was the right size. The right shape...

...and it suited Boa down to the ground.
It was just what he had always wanted.

So if you ever get a present that stinks, say thank you.

Because it might turn out to be...

...the **best** present **ever!**